Garland Cove – Deborah Sheldon
Death In The Dugout – Bruce Harris

Beats! Ballads! Blank Verse!

Book 1: Echoes From An Expired Earth – Allen Ashley
Book 2: Grave Goods – Cardinal Cox
Book 3: From Long Ago – Paul Woodward
Book 4: Laws Of Discord – William Clunie
Book 5: Fanged Dandelion – Eric LaRocca

Weird! Wonderful! Other Worlds

Book 1: The Raven King – Liz Tuckwell
Book 2: The Wired City – Yolanda Sfetsos

Horror Novels & Novellas

House Of Wrax – Raven Dane
And Blood Did Fall – Chad A. Clark
The Fallen – Anthony Watson
The Underclass – Dan Weatherer
Cheslyn Myre – Dan Weatherer
Greenbeard – John Travis
Tower Of Raven – Kevin M. Folliard
Welcome Home Natalie – Reyna Young
Little Bird – TR Hitchman
Society Place – Andrew David Barker
Axe – Terry Grimwood
Wicked Blood – E.C. Hanson
The Again-Walkers – Deborah Sheldon
Between The Teeth Of Charon – Grant Longstaff

Science Fiction Novels & Novellas

Odyssey Of The Black Turtle – Paul Woodward
Sons Of Sol – Kevin R. McNally

The 'A QUIET APOCALYPSE' Series

A Quiet Apocalypse – Dave Jeffery
Cathedral (A Quiet Apocalypse Book 2) – Dave Jeffery
The Samaritan (A Quiet Apocalypse Book 3) – Dave Jeffery
A Silent Dystopia (Stories Of A Quiet Apocalypse) – Edited by D.T. Griffith

General Fiction

Joe – Terry Grimwood
Finding Jericho – Dave Jeffery

Science Fiction Collections

Vistas – Chris Kelso

Horror Fiction Collections

Distant Frequencies – Frank Duffy
Where We Live – Tim Cooke
Night Voices – Paul Edwards & Frank Duffy

Anthologies

The Darkest Battlefield – Tales Of WW1/Horror

DEMAIN PUBLISHING

Short Sharp Shocks!

Book 0: Dirty Paws - Dean M. Drinkel
Book 1: Patient K - Barbie Wilde
Book 2: The Stranger & The Ribbon – Tim Dry
Book 3: Asylum Of Shadows – Stephanie Ellis
Book 4: Monster Beach – Ritchie Valentine Smith
Book 5: Beasties & Other Stories – Martin Richmond
Book 6: Every Moon Atrocious – Emile-Louis Tomas Jouvet
Book 7: A Monster Met – Liz Tuckwell
Book 8: The Intruders & Other Stories – Jason D. Brawn
Book 9: The Other – David Youngquist
Book 10: Symphony Of Blood – Leah Crowley
Book 11: Shattered – Anthony Watson
Book 12: The Devil's Portion – Benedict J. Jones
Book 13: Cinders Of A Blind Man Who Could See – Kev Harrison
Book 14: Dulce Et Decorum Est – Dan Howarth
Book 15: Blood, Bears & Dolls – Allison Weir
Book 16: The Forest Is Hungry – Chris Stanley
Book 17: The Town That Feared Dusk – Calvin Demmer
Book 18: Night Of The Rider – Alyson Faye
Book 19: Isidora's Pawn – Erik Hofstatter
Book 20: Plain – D.T. Griffith
Book 21: Supermassive Black Mass – Matthew Davis
Book 22: Whispers Of The Sea (& Other Stories) – L. R. Bonehill
Book 23: Magic – Eric Nash
Book 24: The Plague – R.J. Meldrum
Book 25: Candy Corn – Kevin M. Folliard
Book 26: The Elixir – Lee Allen Howard
Book 27: Breaking The Habit – Yolanda Sfetsos
Book 28: Forfeit Tissue – C. C. Adams

Book 29: Crown Of Thorns – Trevor Kennedy
Book 30: The Encampment / Blood Memory – Zachary Ashford
Book 31: Dreams Of Lake Drukka / Exhumation – Mike Thorn
Book 32: Apples / Snail Trails – Russell Smeaton
Book 33: An Invitation To Darkness – Hailey Piper
Book 34: The Necessary Evils & Sick Girl – Dan Weatherer
Book 35: The Couvade – Joe Koch
Book 36: The Camp Creeper & Other Stories – Dave Jeffery
Book 37: Flaying Sins – Ian Woodhead
Book 38: Hearts & Bones – Theresa Derwin
Book 39: The Unbeliever & The Intruder – Morgan K. Tanner
Book 40: The Coffin Walk – Richard Farren Barber
Book 41: The Straitjacket In The Woods – Kitty R. Kane
Book 42: Heart Of Stone – M. Brandon Robbins
Book 43: Bits – R.A. Busby
Book 44: Last Meal In Osaka & Other Stories – Gary Buller
Book 45: The One That Knows No Fear – Steve Stred
Book 46: The Birthday Girl & Other Stories – Christopher Beck
Book 47: Crowded House & Other Stories - S.J. Budd
Book 48: Hand To Mouth – Deborah Sheldon
Book 49: Moonlight Gunshot Mallet Flame / A Little Death – Alicia Hilton
Book 50: Dark Corners - David Charlesworth

Murder! Mystery! Mayhem!

Maggie Of My Heart – Alyson Faye
The Funeral Birds – Paula R.C. Readman
Cursed – Paul M. Feeney
The Bone Factory – Yolanda Sfetsos

BETWEEN THE TEETH OF CHARON

BY

GRANT LONGSTAFF

First Published 2022

For further information, please visit:
WEB: www.demainpublishing.com
TWITTER: @DemainPubUk
FACEBOOK: Demain Publishing
INSTAGRAM: demainpublishing

"It is only after one is in trouble that one realizes how little sympathy and kindness there are in the world."

- Nellie Bly, *Ten Days in a Mad-House.*

"There is no great secret. Historically, the treatment of mental health was poor. But what the patients of Hethpool Grange endured, specifically in the final years of operation, was beyond despicable...and, I fear, we may only know a fraction of it."

- Margaret R. Fletcher, *Cruelty and Conditioning: An Oral History of the Laughing Academy*

"One need not be a Chamber—to be Haunted—
One need not be a House—
The Brain has Corridors—surpassing
Material Place—"

- Emily Dickinson, *One need not be a Chamber to be Haunted*

CONTENTS

PART ONE: RUIN – 2020

CHAPTER ONE

Jack stood outside the crematorium and shook each clammy hand forced into his. He heard the echo of sympathies and condolences, whispered his own tired expressions of gratitude. The voices, most of all his own, small and withered in the wake of death. After a silent moment he nodded to each pale faced mourner, indistinct in their coal black uniform of grief, pointed them towards the garden of remembrance then took the next hand.

"She was kind to me when no one else was."

The words jolted Jack from his bleak programming, shocked him into the cold day.

"Ellen," Jack said.

"I'm sorry she's gone."

"Me too."

Ellen reached up to Jack's face, wiped a lone tear away with her thumb.

"Nora wouldn't want you to cry."

"No, she wouldn't."

He became aware of the young woman stood behind Ellen. Her features ghostly echoes from the generations before hers.

"This is—"

"*Dani*," Jack interrupted Ellen, "I knew your father. You look just like him. I was sorry to hear about his death."

Dani nodded once then looked intently at the ground between her feet, as if hoping it might split open and swallow her whole. Jack understood. He was waiting for a black chasm of his own.

Ellen gently touched his shoulder.

"How are you holding up?" Ellen said.

"I'm okay," Jack said.

"Liar."

"*Nanna*," Dani said.

"Oh please," Ellen said, "he can lie to these other folks but not to me."

Ellen knew death better than most. It had taken the man she loved. Their only child. The woman was steeped in tragedy. Jack marvelled at the fire, the fight, still burning bright in her eyes.

"I hope I can find the same strength as you."

"You will. For Nora. You have to."

It was Jack's turn to look at the ground. He swallowed something hard, invisible. He felt the tears on his cheeks, watched as they burst softly on the solid, unyielding earth.

***

Once the procession of mourners passed, Jack stood in the shadows of the grey crematorium, away from the bright, winter sun. He was not yet ready for the harsh colours of the bouquets and wreaths which covered the pavement below a plastic plaque adorned with his wife's name.

Nora.

Later, the name would be scrubbed away, the already wilting flowers mulched into compost, Nora's body reduced to nothing but ash.

Everything was temporary, except death.

Only a handful of people remained in the memorial garden. No one wanted to be around death longer than was absolutely necessary. Jack felt the tension in his shoulders slip away. Soon he could leave and return to his private nightmare. He was not ungrateful, but the sincere kindness and warmth of others hurt. He welcomed the return of the void.

"Sir?"

Jack closed his eyes, took a readying breath, turned to the voice.

The man standing before Jack was old. *Ancient.*

"Hello," Jack said, "were you—I don't think I saw you inside."

"No."

The man's eyes buzzed from side to side, struggling to focus. He fidgeted with the knot of his tie, loose around his neck, with trembling fingers.

"Sorry, do I know you?"

"Yes. Once. Some time ago."

Jack stared at the stranger, hoping his memory would snag on some faint thread of recognition.

"I'm sorry. At my age—"

"Hethpool Grange."

"What?"

"You and Nora. You worked there."

"Yes," Jack shook his head. "That was a long time ago."

"Coyne."

The air around Jack thickened, became difficult to breathe. *Coyne*. His heart was beating too fast.

"Why are you here?"

"He's here," the man tapped a crooked finger against his temple. "In my head. I can feel him in my dreams. Reaching out for me, calling me back."

"Listen, Coyne—"

"He's still out there."

"—is dead."

"I can feel his eyes on me. Like furnaces of fire."

There was a familiarity in the deep lines of the man's face, his eyes.

"You're mistaken. Coyne is dead."

Jack's vision became watery and the relentless hammering in his chest intensified. He turned, staggered away from the stranger.

No. You know him.

The world was spinning, flashes of colour and light dancing with long shadows. A far-off part of Jack hoped he was dying.

"Jack."

Hands seized his shoulders, stopped him colliding into the earth. He looked up, blinked his eyes clear.

The man was gone.

"Are you okay?" Dani was holding him upright, eyes fixed on his.

"I'm fine, I..." Jack took a deep breath to smother the burning in his lungs, "I'm okay."

"Who was that?" Ellen said, looking past Jack into the empty space behind him.

"No idea."

"What did he say?"

Coyne. Jack shook his head. *He's still out there.*

"Nothing. I'm tired, that's all. I haven't been sleeping, and all of this..."

Jack fell silent. *This*. This was easy to say. Easier than the truth buried within it.

"Come on," Dani said, "let's get you home."

***

Ellen and Dani insisted on taking Jack inside despite his objections. At seventy-eight, he knew when the fight was lost. The women followed him through the garden, watched patiently as he fished the key from his pocket, waited politely to be invited inside. Jack led them into the living room.

"Thank you both," Jack said, then added, "I should make some tea."

"No," Ellen said, "we should go. I just wanted to see you home."

Dani excused herself to use the bathroom leaving Ellen and Jack alone. A heavy silence pushed into the space between them, palpable as the quiet before a shootout in those old westerns, as they listened to Dani climb the stairs and move out of earshot. Distantly a door closed, a bolt slid home.

Ellen, quick as ever, shot first.

"Who was it?"

"I don't know."

"Jack, I saw your face, how it changed."

There was no fooling Ellen. There never had been.

"I think it was, Ollie," Jack said.

"*Ollie?* That must make him close to a hundred years old."

"He knew I had worked at Hethpool Grange. He mentioned..."

The unspoken name soured Jack's mouth. Ellen put a hand to her throat, pinched the skin with her thumb and forefinger.

"Coyne," Ellen's eyes were glassy. "Why?"

"I have no idea. He said something about him, Coyne, still being there. Said he could feel his eyes on him."

"That's not possible."

"No."

Ellen sucked her lower lip into her mouth, released it with a pop.

"This isn't fair. Not today."

"Ellen, what I did..."

"You ready, Nanna?" Dani said.

The invisible dark between Jack and Ellen diminished and light returned.

Later, after the women left him alone, Jack returned to his empty world.

CHAPTER TWO

The days collapsed into one another and nights lingered as long as winter.

Jack no longer recognised the home he and Nora had shared for most of their marriage. A ceaseless draught he hadn't known before now stalked the house. All light was dulled beneath gathering dust. What sounds broke the quiet were distant, muted, false. The rooms, bleached of all their colour and life, were filled with the spectre of memory.

Grief was a haunted house.

Only Nora—every sweet and beautiful part of her—was gone forever and there is no such thing as ghosts.

***

The phone ringing shattered the glassy silence.

The shrill peal seemed to make the air in the room tremble, threatening to rupture the comforting thrum of the muted television. Jack wasn't sure how long he had sat in front of the screen, bathed in the vivid flashes of colour from a game-show, but he guessed it was hours. Time, like everything else, was changed.

The day outside was moving towards purple twilight. He took a sip from his forgotten coffee, swallowed the bitter swill.

He made no attempt to go to the phone, had stopped answering it after the undertaker had called a third time to ask when Jack would stop by to collect Nora's ashes.

***

When the phone screamed for a third time that evening, Jack relented.

He lifted the receiver, lies readied to appease whatever platitude might be offered so he could return to his hollow.

"Hello?"

"Jack? It's Ellen," a pause, "how are you?"

Jack closed his eyes and rubbed a hand over the bristles of stubble on his chin and cheeks. He tried to remember when he last shaved, couldn't. There was no lie he could tell which would hide the bleak truth.

"Completely lost."

They spoke for ten minutes or so, negotiating the comfortable terrain of pleasantries. Jack felt human again, grounded, surprised by the peace afforded by small talk. Then the conversation reached a natural summit and they both fell quiet.

"It was good talking, Ellen."

"Wait," Ellen said.

"What is it?"

"I'm going back."

"Where?"

Jack asked the question but already knew the answer.

"Hethpool Grange."

"Ellen—"

"I keep thinking about Nora's funeral. About Ollie and what he said. I want rid of this shadow hanging over me. I want to tell Dani."

"Tell her what? No good will come of it."

There was a crackle on the line. A sigh. A groan. Jack couldn't tell.

"Years ago, when Owen was still a boy, I asked Nora if I should tell him about Pete. She didn't give me an answer, you know how she was. Only *I* knew the answer, all that stuff. But she promised, if I ever decided to tell Owen about his father, she would help me."

"But you never did?"

"No. Life makes a habit of getting in the way. I'm old. I don't know how long I have. Now, I can't tell Owen about his dad, but I can tell Dani about her grandfather."

"But why go back?"

"Because Pete is out there. In a shallow grave beneath an unmarked stone."

Something stirred in the recesses of Jack's heart. Black memories, buried deep, crawled from their lightless cells.

"Help me tell her," Ellen said.

Jack thought Ellen might be crying.

"I'm sorry. I can't."

"*Jack.*"

Jack hung up the phone.

***

Jack awoke on the sofa, his heart beating hard and fast, the nightmare lingering in reality. He closed his eyes, tried to recall where he had been moments before.

There was only fog and guilt, ash and terror.

He lay there for hours, navigating a maze of cheerless memories, until the grey, early morning light soaked up the shadows and calmed the pulsing muscle in his chest.

Later that afternoon, Jack picked up the phone.

"Hello?"
"I'll do it," Jack said. "For Nora."

CHAPTER THREE

The three of them—Jack, Ellen and Dani—sat around the small table in Ellen's kitchen.

"So, what's this about?" Dani said over the mug of black coffee steaming in her hands, eyes hawkish, impatient.

"I want to tell you something," Ellen said.

"Oh," Dani's gaze danced between Ellen and Jack, "are you two in some kind of twilight-of-life romance? Because, that's totally fine, but you don't need to sit me down and tell me about it. And don't tell me the two of you are having—"

"We're not."

"Not together? Or having sex?"

The beginning of a smile touched the corner of Jack's mouth.

"Neither. *Christ.*" Ellen dropped her eyes. "Dani, I need you to listen to me. I need to tell you about my life. There are parts of it, dark parts, I buried deep."

"Nanna, you're scaring me."

"Hush now and listen."

Ellen took Dani's hands. The knot of their knuckles reminded Jack of a heart. Warm, full of love. It hurt to look at it. Then Ellen was talking, dragging the past to the present, and there was no way back.

"My mother left my father when I was ten. He was a miserable man, to both her and me. She didn't take me with her and I've done my time contemplating why. Why doesn't matter. What matters is, she left. I became what my father called *wayward*. Which meant I was a little shit. As soon as I turned sixteen, he took me to a mental hospital and had me committed. I didn't see him again."

"Jesus," Dani said.

"They pumped me so full of drugs I don't know if I cared. I floated around like a ghost lost in fog. Hethpool Grange is where I met Nora and Jack. She was a nurse and kind when no one else was. I met a boy too, another patient. Peter. Pete. He was a month older. Quiet, shy. He could tell you the name of any bird—the proper, Latin ones—which happened upon our little corner of hell. We became friends and fell in love sometime later. The head physician, a man named Coyne, took a shine to me, liked to take me into his office."

Ellen's voice cracked, clipped her speech.

"Nanna?" Dani said. "What are you saying?"

"Not that. It wasn't that. He would talk about stuff I didn't understand, would rest his hand on my knee or rub my shoulder as he did. Men like that..." Ellen paused, calculated her words. "Everything he said came down to one thing. Power. I was afraid of him. Women didn't talk back then and no one would have believed a girl from the nuthouse. But Nora, she did. And she did her best to keep me away from him.

"I fell pregnant. Stolen moments with Pete in the laundry room. Anyway, when I told him, he seemed to come alive. He wanted to be a dad, and a good one. We planned to run away together. Stupid given we were sixteen and knew nothing of the world. You will never make plans as lovely as those you make when you are young and in love.

"Of course, Coyne found out. He killed Pete. He never got to meet his son. Your dad. What Coyne did, not just to us, but to the people at Hethpool...the man was a monster."

"What happened to him?" Dani said, her voice quiet.

"There was a fire at the hospital. Coyne died."

Jack watched a tear roll down Ellen's cheek. He thought he might feel some peace in hearing the words spoken aloud and no longer whispered. But there was none. The old wounds split open and spilled new pain.

***

"Thank you," Ellen said.

Jack and Ellen were alone in the kitchen. Dani had gone upstairs to change.

"I didn't do anything," Jack said.

"You were here. That was enough."

"You still sure you want to go back?" Jack asked.

"Did Dani put you up to this?"

"No, of course not."

"You must think I'm mad?"

"We don't use that word around here."

Jack smiled as he repeated his wife's words from long ago. The gesture alien on his face.

"God, I can't count how many times she said that," Ellen sighed, seemed to grow smaller. Jack knew the invisible weight. "I need to go back. I can feel it, like it's calling out to me."

"Ollie said the same thing," Jack said.

"I suppose we'll always carry it with us. I'll be seventy-five soon. I feel the age in my bones. If I don't do this now, whilst I still can, I worry I'll never do it."

The two of them sat in silence for a moment.

"You didn't tell Dani I started the fire," Jack said.

"*We* started the fire, Jack. You, me, Nora. We all did it."

***

The morning was clear and cold and would be colder again once they were in the hills. No one had spoken since leaving Ellen's flat, the weight of the past still heavy on their hearts. A tangle of thorns formed in Jack's chest sometime after they left Newcastle, the quiet feeding the anxious barbs prickling his insides as he drove. He thumbed on the radio somewhere past Morpeth to lessen the subdued mood in the car. The music—Jack thought it might be Kate Bush, singing of sleep and sheep—shattered the bleak malaise almost immediately.

Dani spoke up from the back seat.

"Where is it?"

"Up in the Cheviots," Jack said, "middle of nowhere really."

"Back then they didn't know what to do with people like me, like Pete. Far easier to hide us someplace we could easily be forgotten," Ellen said.

Dani reached between the seats, laid a hand on Ellen's shoulder.

"Are you sure you want to do this?"

"Yes."

In Ellen's lap was a small bunch of daffodils—yellow petals surrounding their cream cornets—the kind Pete would pick from the edge of the hospital grounds and present to Ellen. The sentiment, so small, so terribly precious, was almost too much for Jack.

His heart was shattered. His life somehow less than empty. But Jack and Nora had been given something precious. *Time*. Time to hold one another. Time to kiss the tears from each other's knuckles. Time to say goodbye.

Coyne had robbed Ellen of any such peace.

Jack flexed his hands on the wheel, pushed the accelerator, watched the car swallow tarmac and race into memory.

***

It was more than fifty years since Jack took the road to Hethpool Grange, but the bends and turns came back to him with familiar ease. The hills on either side, a palate of winter green and brown, were unchanged. What grew seemed wilder now, barbed and twisted in the brutal expanse, limbs and leaves sucking the light from the sky to cast the earth in a sunless grey.

It was along this road Jack and Nora fell in love. He could still recall the morning sun on her face as dawn broke and later, on the tired drive home, how she would rest her hand on his. Sometimes, on hot, cloudless nights when their passion could not be stilled, he would park the car by the road and lose himself in the beauty of Nora, her face, her body, framed with stars. After making love they would lie together on the bonnet of Jack's old Austin Cambridge, naked, bathing in the cool night breeze, watching hares dance and play in the moonlight.

"We'll have a bunny of our own one day," Nora promised, pressing a hand to the pale flesh of her stomach.

Only the bunny they both longed for never came.

"Are you okay?" Ellen said.

"Fine," Jack said, realising he was crying, "remembering Nora, that's all."

After leaving the main road, Jack navigated a narrow dirt track, forgotten by the world. The lane, hidden beneath the limbs of old trees, ended at a wall of climbing weeds and sickly ivy. A row of rusted iron teeth, biting into the swollen sky beyond the branches, marked the old hospital gate. Jack looked up at the fangs, switched off the engine.

"Here we are."

"This place was always worst when it was quiet," Ellen said.

"Why?" Dani said.

"The screaming and crying kept you up all night—but it let you know there was someone else out there."

***

The gate jerked open when Jack put his weight against it, the wall of vines splitting as the ancient hinges whined in their brackets. He motioned to Ellen and Dani with his free hand, watched them slip inside. Once the women had passed, he followed them into the grounds.

Hethpool Grange stood a few hundred meters before them, looming out of the murky sky. It dominated the landscape. The towers on either side of the administration building, imposing and resolute, stood guard over the wings—the east and what remained of the west—which stretched off to either side. The red brick was now the colour of clotted blood, the sandstone window frames slick with decades of grime. The roof above was a range of treacherous peaks, the shattered slates smothered in vivid algae.

"There they stand, imperious," Jack said.

"What?" Dani asked.

Jack opened his mouth to speak, stopped when the sun broke through the clouds beyond the hospital and birthed its shadow. For a long moment it reached towards them, stretched like fingers creeping closer, threatening to pull them from the light and into the gloom, before the clouds blotted out the light once more.

A breath Jack didn't know he was holding escaped his lungs.

"It's nothing," Jack said, "come on."

They walked around the long-abandoned gardens, now overrun with thick weeds and brambles, and climbed the slight rise to the left of the east wing. It was a longer route to the graveyard, and they were slowed by age and the uneven earth beneath them, but it ensured they kept their distance from the hospital and its shadow, should it return.

They stopped at the first row of small, flat stones, each framed with long, dead grass, without a word. Jack looked at the marker by his feet, tried to decipher the engraving on the surface, could only make out the faintest of scars. Whoever lay beneath his feet was lost, scrubbed away by the relentless wind and rain. Beside him, Dani spoke.

"Jesus. How many people are buried out here?"

Jack shook his head. He didn't know, didn't want to.

"Come on," Ellen said, "Pete is over there."

***

Ellen guided them through the stones, stopping by a tree on the far side of the field. Jack and Dani watched Ellen move beneath the canopy of twisted limbs and touch the wide trunk. Slowly, she ran her pale, trembling fingers over the cracked bark, as though tracing the lines in the face of a lover.

"Nanna?"

Ellen looked back at Jack and Dani, smiled as best she could.

"Give me a moment alone, would you?"

***

Jack and Dani left Ellen alone with her grief, stopping once they reached the edge of the graveyard and were far enough away from the dead. The sky overhead had darkened, swollen with lead-coloured clouds. The rising wind caught in the tall pines and filled the day with a constant moan like static on an old TV.

"Hopefully we'll beat the rain," Jack said.

"What was he like?" Dani said. "Pete?"

Her eyes fixed on Jack's.

"He was a good man," Jack said.

It was a poor summation of a life, but it was all he could manage.

"I know it doesn't matter, not really, but I have to ask. Why was he here?"

"Manic depression. I suppose it would be bipolar nowadays. He was sectioned for trying to commit suicide, but Pete didn't belong here. Most people didn't. This place—"

"What is it?"

"I knew it was bad—with Coyne, I mean—but I didn't realise how bad. Not until Pete. I was too late in..."

Shame and guilt came alive within Jack, crawling beneath his skin with insectile haste. The anxiety Jack had come to know intimately squeezed against his ribs. He pushed a hand to his chest, trying to placate the familiar pain he had carried most of his life.

"Hey," Dani's hand squeezed his, warm and firm, "this isn't your fault. None of it."

"That's kind of you to say, but I've had fifty odd years to think on it. There hasn't been a day I haven't thought about this place and how it changed our lives. I've never been able to let it go. It's like there's this profound sadness in me, an emptiness I can't seem to shake."

"That's awful."

"Sometimes it is. If it wasn't for Nora," Jack sighed, "I should have done more, and sooner. It was Nora and your grandmother who stopped Coyne. They were stronger than I ever have been."

"I hate to think how I would have turned out without her. Especially after Dad. She was amazing."

"She's a tough, old bird."

"That she is. Just don't let her hear you calling her old."

"Dani, I need you to do something?"

"What?"

"When this is done, I don't think I can see Ellen again. It's too much. Just, look after her okay?"

Quiet—the peaceful kind which always seemed to follow an expulsion of hidden feeling—came then. Jack closed his eyes and listened to the whispering pines, wondered what they spoke to one another, hoped they had forgotten the pain and blood which soaked their roots.

"Oh God."

It was Ellen.

Jack saw the daffodils somersaulting in the wind, Ellen's arm, stretched towards Hethpool Grange, the horror on Dani's face. He turned to the hospital.

Ollie stood in the empty frame of a third story window, rocking unsteadily in the wind, staring down at them.

I can feel him...

"He's going to jump," Jack said.

...in my head.

Jack was moving towards the hospital, hands out in front of him, pleading.

"Ollie, don't do this. Please, don't do this."

Ollie looked over his shoulder, into the dark room behind him, and nodded. He turned his face to the bitter sky, raised his arms like he might try to fly.

"No."

Jack watched Ollie fall through the gloom like a dropped marionette.

CHAPTER FOUR

Jack was kneeling in a deepening pool of vivid blood. He took Ollie's hand, squeezed the limp fingers as the crimson soaked through his trousers and cooled against his knees.

"Stay with me. Stay with me, now."

Ollie blinked slowly and tried to speak, coughing instead. Jack felt a fine, crimson mist speckle his cheeks and lips. He fought the urge to wipe his face clean and turned to Dani.

"Call an ambulance."

"What?"

"Dani? Dani, look at me."

Jack waited for her frantic eyes to settle on his, focus.

"He's—"

"Dani, keep looking at me okay?" Jack kept his voice quiet, tried to still the tremor in his throat. "Good. Stay with me. Good."

"Is he dead?"

"I need you to phone an ambulance. Okay? Dani, can you do that?"

Dani nodded slowly, fingers slipping into the pocket of her jeans. Jack turned back to Ollie.

"We'll get you an ambulance. Get you to a hospital."

"*No*."

"Quiet now, don't speak."

"No signal," Dani said.

Ollie grabbed Jack's coat with his free hand and pulled him close.

"*Still...*" Ollie managed, his voice a watery whisper.

He's still out there.

"I can't get a signal."

The muscles in Ollie's face slackened. The tension in his fractured body eased as his life slipped away.

"He's dead," Jack said.

Blood, thick and black, ran from Ollie's mouth.

"Jack?" Ellen said.

"He's gone, Ellen."

"*Jack.*"

Jack turned. Ellen was not looking at the body but the hospital, towering above. Her gaze danced over the old stones, sharp and feverish, as though searching for something lost.

"What is it?" Jack said.

"Nanna?"

"He was pushed," Ellen said, "I saw him."

Her eyes bore into Jack, insisting on the truth in her words. Panic seized him, wrapped him in its sickly arms and squeezed the breath from his lungs.

Don't say it.

"I swear it was him. *It was Coyne*."

***

"We need to leave. Now." Ellen said.

Jack stood quickly, ignoring the split of pain deep in his knees as he did so. He closed the gap between himself and the women.

"We can't just leave," Dani said, "we need to wait for help."

"No. We have to go," Ellen said.

"Nanna, he fell."

"We can get help once we're at the car."

"You said Coyne was dead."

"I know, I—"

"Whatever you think you saw, it wasn't that, it couldn't have been. Jack, please?"

Dani looked from her grandmother to Jack, pushed her open palms towards him in a plea for support.

"Your Gran's right."

"This isn't right," Dani said. Voice quiet in defeat.

"We can call for help when we're on the road."

Betrayal complete, Jack turned to the horizon, to the darkening clouds which shrouded the distant hills. The wind shrieked around them, cried against the strong walls of Hethpool Grange, the smell of burning heavy on its breath. A moment later, a grey flurry filled the air above and surrendered to the chill breeze as it drifted towards the listless earth.

Jack opened his hand to the sky.

"It that snow?" Dani said.

A grey flake landed in his palm. Jack pushed a finger against the delicate offering, drew a steel-coloured smudge over the deep lines of his palm. Jack watched Ellen put her own hand into the dust, saw the grey powder settle into the curls of Dani's hair.

"It's ash," Jack said.

***

By the time they reached the front of the hospital the world was smothered in a fine sheet of monochrome ash. They navigated the old gardens, what little colour it still held now lost, bleached a morbid charcoal. Jack followed Ellen and Dani between the crumbling edging of the forgotten flowerbeds, stopping behind the women at the edge of the garden. Ellen coughed. A single, raw bark followed with a series of dry heaves as she choked on the ash.

"How much further?" Dani said.

Jack glanced over his shoulder, squinting at the spectral shape of the hospital in the thickening ash, turned back to the whirling cinders ahead.

"Still a bit to go," Jack said. His lungs burned with fatigue.

"Fuck," Dani said.

"I'm okay." Ellen coughed again, back curling as she searched for a real breath. Dani grabbed her grandmother, rubbed her back to soothe Ellen's lungs.

They needed to get out of the storm. Out of the ash. Jack glared into the frantic murk, saw the small group of outbuildings to their right. He pointed towards the building nearest to them. An old storage shed.

"Over there," Jack said, swallowing a mouthful of bitter air.

"*No*. We need to get away from this place," Ellen said.

She was crying, her tears clearing a path through the pallid dust on her face.

"You need to take it easy, Nanna." Ellen made to protest, sputtered. "Don't talk. It'll help keep this shit out of your lungs. Come on."

***

Jack closed the door of the shed against the torrent of ash and pressed his forehead to the damp wood. He grimaced at the cool slime against his brow, heaved in a breath of earth and rot. He closed his eyes, allowed his lungs to gorge themselves on the moulding air, feed his starving heart.

"Ash doesn't fall from the sky," Dani said.

Jack listened to the swell of the wind outside. Soothed by the ambient, almost indistinct tremors which pushed at the door, he lost himself in silent contemplation. After a time, he turned and spoke.

"No. But, it happened," Jack said, "*is* happening."

It was all he could think to say. Dani and Ellen glanced at each other, faces ghostly in the thin, grey light seeping through the single window. Jack waited for their silent communication to end.

"It's happening," Ellen said.

"Okay. It's happening," Dani shook her head, slowly. "So, what do we do?"

"Do you have a signal?"

Dani lifted her phone, absently wiped the ash from the screen.

"None."

"Okay. *Shit*. Okay. You wait here—I'll go get the car, bring it up."

"What about the gate?" Ellen said.

"It's an old lock. A nudge with the car should do it."

"I'll go," Dani said.

"No, you stay here," Jack said.

"Don't take this the wrong way, but you shouldn't be out in that stuff either. You're both—"

"Old?" Ellen smiled.

"I was going to say vulnerable."

"Vulnerable? Jesus. I'll take old over vulnerable any day," Ellen sighed. "However, she's right, Jack. We're vulnerable."

Ellen winked at Dani. Jack raised his hands.

"I'm not going to argue."

"Just as well. It won't do any good," Dani said.

Jack took out the key fob and tossed it to Dani.

"She's got your blood, Ellen."

Dani pushed the key into the front of her jeans and wound her scarf free from her neck. Jack watched as she shook dust from the flimsy material, revealing a pattern of pastel pink doves against a lilac sky then made a series of folds until the scarf was a triangle. She pulled the cloth over her nose and mouth, tied the corners at the back of her head. Makeshift mask complete, she headed for the door.

"Be careful out there," Ellen said.

"I will."

"And if you get a signal, call an ambulance. The police."

Dani stopped, her hand firm on the rusted handle.

"Nanna, you said he was dead. What you think you saw—"

"It *was* him."

Ellen turned to the window in an effort to hide her tears but the daylight caught them and turned them into silver orbs. Pain for all the world to see. Ellen spoke again.

"I know it doesn't make any sense, that I sound..." Ellen shook her head.

Jack knew those unspoken words, understood the suffering they caused.

"Nanna?"

"Believe me, the irony of where we are isn't lost on me. This place. It gets inside your head. It's been almost sixty years, but I feel some part of me never left. Do you know how often I wonder, if what I lost back then, was every bit of good in me?"

"That's not true. What about Dad? What about me?"

Ellen wiped away the tears with the back of her hand, pressed her fingers against her neck.

"I saw Coyne—something like him—in that window."

Jack wiped away a tear itching the stubble on his cheek and nodded. He believed Ellen, believed she saw Coyne push Ollie. He pushed his hands into the pockets of his jacket and squeezed them into tight fists, but still they trembled.

***

Jack waited until he and Ellen were alone before he spoke again.

"When you saw Coyne, you said you saw something *like* him. What did you mean?"

"Good god, I don't know anymore," Ellen said. She was still by the window, lost in the pale landscape beyond the pane.

"Talk me through what you saw."

"Do you think I'm mad?"

"No. Never."

Ellen turned from the window and offered Jack a fragile, momentary, smile before grave concern returned.

"I saw a figure behind Ollie. A black shape, even in all that darkness. It was him."

"But, Coyne?"

"Do you believe in ghosts?"

"What? No, I—"

"Me either. But I could feel his eyes on me, watching me like he used to back then."

"I watched him die."

"I know. But I know what I saw..."

Jack was silent. He pressed a hand to a fresh ache in his temple as his skull weathered the onslaught of nightmare images. He closed his eyes on the past. Waited for the storm to pass.

"Shit," Jack shook his head, "I believe you."

***

The sound of a car engine broke the quiet in the shed and a moment later Jack and Ellen were back amongst the ash.

Dani was out of the car and heading down the wide drive beyond the flowerbeds, closing the distance between them. She thrust a chamois leather into her grandmother's hand. Ellen took the cloth and pushed it against her mouth and nose as Dani took her by the arm.

"It was all I could find," Dani said.

With his eyes to the ashen earth in an effort to shield himself from the soot, Jack stumbled ahead of the women, stopping when a moan, low and hoarse, rose behind him. He raised his head, ready to turn back to the women, stopped.

Something stood near the car.

The figure loomed, coal black amongst the swirling whites and greys. The features were lost in the darkness of it, the daylight unable to find the nuance of humanity, leaving only the black cut-out of a torso and limbs.

Jack took in the size of it.

Of him.

Coyne.

The air around Jack seemed to vibrate, shifting the figure in and out of focus, liquified in a heat shimmer. Only it was not the air causing the mirage. The heat emanated from the silhouette. Jack saw onyx flakes of charred, paper thin flesh, peel away from Coyne's body, watched them rise and dance on the invisible currents of air. Jack was unable to move, mesmerised by the burning shape before him.

"No," Jack muttered, a feeble denial of the sight before him, "No. *No*."

Tears spilled down his cheeks as Coyne reached out towards the driver's side tyre. The movement was slow, laboured, the hallmark of old pains Jack knew all too well. Coyne pressed something thin against the rubber of the tyre. A moment of resistance then a loud sigh as compressed air rushed out into the world. The hissing broke Jack's malaise.

"Go. Move. *Now.*" Jack shouted.

Jack turned, saw Ellen and Dani were already moving away from Coyne. He followed as quickly as age would allow, ribs crushing his lungs filled with dry, lifeless air. He pushed a coat sleeve to his mouth and nose as a makeshift filter and moved towards Hethpool Grange.

Jack caught up to the women on the wide stone porch as he mounted the stairs and pushed the double doors. The right-side door lurched inwards, its base scraping over the tiles of the foyer. Once they were in the gloom of the hospital, Jack took a final glance outside.

Coyne stalked towards them through the ash; his pace slow, assiduous.

Jack slammed the door on the terror which hunted him and shut them into the ruins of the past.

CHAPTER FIVE

Jack pressed his back to the door, his breathing ragged. He ran a hand over his forehead, wiped away the tickling beads of sweat. There was a dull scraping in the shadows beyond the stairs, then Dani emerged with something which looked like a bundle of sticks in her arms.

"Here."

Dani dropped her haul in the centre of the foyer. A discordant clang of metal against metal filled the space and rippled up the thick walls of the hospital. Jack looked at the dropped sticks, realised they were iron spindles from the staircase.

"To jamb the door," Dani explained, "Nanna?"

Ellen stood on the far side of the foyer at the foot of the imperial staircase which climbed into the gloom above them. Her expression vacant, eerily familiar inside these walls. Her mind slipping away from the awful reality.

"*Nanna?*"

"Huh?"

"Stay with us," Dani said.

Jack lifted one of the spindles and fed it through the 'D' shaped handles on the double doors, twisting the makeshift bar so it was tight between the wood and metal.

"I'm not sure this will work," Jack said.

Beside him, Dani stooped, stabbed a spindle into the small space between the bottom of the door and the floor. She kicked it home, hard, the makeshift chock wedged firm. Jack joined her to secure the other door.

"Will it hold?" Ellen said.

Jack was pleased to see the sleepy glaze had left her eyes and given way to bright urgency.

"I hope so," Jack said, "but we need to—"

Dani pressed a finger to her lips, commanding quiet.

Jack waited in the dense silence. No. Not silence. Not completely. A noise from the other side of the door. Faint as a breath. The gentle kiss of flames eating kindling.

Outside something burned.

Ellen pointed in the direction of the east wing and took slow steps towards the deeper parts of the hospital, motioning for Jack and Dani to do the same.

"I can smell you, bitch."

The voice outside was stone grinding, soot choked.

Jack moved away from the door, allowed himself to be swallowed by the hungry shadows of Hethpool Grange.

"Is that you, Jacky-boy? Where is your pretty wife?"

Coyne screamed beyond the barred door, the agonising growl of a dying animal. The air around Jack seemed to tremble at the thunderous inferno of hate and rage.

Hell was cold and empty.

The demon was here and it was coming for them.

PART TWO: EMBER - 1963

CHAPTER ONE

"Stop the car," Nora said.

"What?" Jack said.

"Please, stop the car."

The road was deserted but Jack flicked on the indicator anyway, squeezed the brake and bumped the car into the wild grass by the road. He was afraid to look at Nora. If he saw her crying, saw painful tears shining in her eyes, it would shatter his own feeble resolve. Instead, he watched ghostly fingers of vapour curl and stretch in the stark, white light of the headlamps ahead.

"We have to do something," Nora said.

Jack heard her sniff in the dark beside him. He laid his head against the cool glass of the window and closed his eyes. Pete was waiting for him, hanging in the dark of his mind. Dead at the end of a rope. Ellen gently pushing the shoe, loosened when the noose bit into Pete's neck, back onto his bare foot.

"I have an idea. Jack?"

Nora took Jack's hand, pulled him gently back to the present.

"I can see him. Every time I close my eyes he's there." Jack pushed a hand over his eyes to catch the tears spilling from them, sobbed into his palm. "I'm sorry. I—"

"Me too," Nora said, her own voice wavering with hurt, "me too."

They folded into one another, collapsed into their grief.

***

Jack and Nora leaned against the bonnet of the car, their hips pressed together. The only light a faint red ember from the Woodbine they shared, a momentary flare when one of them took a drag. The warm night was filled with delicate sounds. The quiet hiss of the burning cigarette, something tiny moving in the long grass, insects clicking.

"So peaceful," Nora said.

Jack heard the weight of the day, all of Nora's anger and fear, in her soft voice. He took a final pull on the Woodbine, dropped the butt, snuffed out the light with his boot. Where did they go from here? He looked into the clear sky overhead, at the dead and dying stars glinting in the vast night. His insignificance seemed so absolute beneath the expanse of space. It would be easy to surrender to it. He rubbed his tired eyes. Shut out the stars.

"You said you had an idea," Jack said.

"Yes, I," Nora paused, "You want to hear it?"

"God knows."

"If it isn't us, then who? Jack, nobody cares. Coyne is—"

"I know what he's doing. *Christ*."

"We're meant to help these people. We still can. Some of them."

"I know."

"Coyne is evil. Beyond evil. Sister Freeman is besotted with him. And the rest of them, they either don't care or are too afraid to say anything. It's us. It has to be us."

"Tell me."

Nora let out a long sigh beside Jack.

"We take this to the 'papers."

"No, this is—"

"We get a camera and take photos of Hethpool. Of the conditions the patients are kept in, the abuse if we can. Show the world what it's like."

"What makes you think anyone will care?"

"That creep, Powell? He made his big speech to parliament two years ago. He said there would be changes; that places like Hethpool Grange were a thing of the past. What's happening is on people like him too."

"The 'papers may not see it that way."

"I don't care, let them spin it however they wish, I just want to stop Coyne."

Jack lit another cigarette, listened to the insect symphony all around them in the starlit dark. It was not a night he deserved but one he was given none the less. He thought of Pete, naked and alone on a rough slab in the deadhouse, eyes bulging and bloody. Sleeping without stars.

Nora lay her head against Jack's shoulder, took the Woodbine from him. He kissed her forehead, breathed in familiar scents of sweet tobacco and the fading lacquer in her hair. Pete would never know the safety and warmth of moments so ordinary they are forgotten before they can be remembered.

It was not fair.

"We'll have to be careful," Jack said.

"I know."

"I love you."

"I love you, too."

CHAPTER TWO

Jack parked the car in the shadow of the perimeter wall and stopped the engine, the shade swift in smothering the warm September sun overhead.

The air which slipped through the open window, fresh and pine scented, was a blessing inside the stifling car.

"I don't like this," Jack said, "not a bit."

Nora sat beside him, eyes closed as the breeze soothed her baking skin. She held the camera loose in her lap. A Minolta. Slim and silver, small enough to fit into a pocket of her tunic. They made sure of it before leaving Newcastle.

Nora opened her eyes, looked at him apologetically.

"I can go more places than you without anyone questioning me. You know it makes sense."

It did. Still, it didn't mean he had to like it.

Nora slipped the camera into her pocket and sunk into her chair. She looked into the wing mirror, adjusted her cap and the hair held up behind it, made to open the door.

"Wait," Jack said.

"What is it?"

"Nothing, just," Jack swallowed, "be careful, okay?"

"I will."

Jack and Nora left the car and walked together. As they made their way out from beneath the gloomy canopy of trees, Hethpool Grange revealed itself. An ominous, black place. Even in the cold light of day.

Hours later, it burned.

***

After loading the last of the dirty sheets into the huge drum, Jack closed the heavy door and switched on the machine. A second or two passed before the washer lurched into life. There was a slosh of water from inside, then a deafening whirr as the motor began to grind and churn. He left the machine to rinse god only knew what from the sheets and escaped the oppressive damp of the laundry room for a cigarette.

The sun was sinking into the horizon, the blue sky giving way to the encroaching indigo of night. Jack looked at the hospital, thought of Nora. His hands trembled as he thumbed the lighter and lit the Woodbine. Where was she? He hadn't seen her all day, which wasn't unusual, but he would occasionally catch a glimpse of her in the gardens or at the end of a corridor. He would wave and she would smile. A kind, loving smile. One which showed her *goodness* to the world.

"—have one of those, sir?"

The voice startled Jack. Ollie, one of the older patients, limped closer, wincing at some old war wound as he did. Jack handed Ollie his cigarette, lit a fresh one for himself.

"You shouldn't be out here," Jack winked.

"No, sir. But I suppose there's lots of places I shouldn't have been."

"I know."

"Saw lots I shouldn't see too. In France. Mud turned red with all that blood. Us and the krauts? We all bleed the same."

Ollie's eyes became glassy, the horrors of war still raw and alive in his mind.

"Don't think about it," Jack said. It was a paltry thing to say but he had little else.

Ollie nodded at the building behind them.

"Louder than a tank that thing." Ollie offered a toothless smile, then his face collapsed, wrinkled at some remembered darkness. "Saw stuff here too. Doctors put people in those washers. Boiled them right up. Course, that stopped a little while ago, but people still come and go, come and go. We don't matter, not like you."

"You matter, Ollie." Jack felt the hair on his arms, the back of his neck, rise. *Pete mattered*. "You *all* matter."

***

Nora was waiting for Jack by the car. When she saw him emerge from between the pines she began to cry and rushed towards him. He folded his arms around her, pulled her tight against his body.

"Jesus, you're freezing. How long have you been out here?" Jack said. He rubbed her back and arms in an effort to restore the stolen warmth.

"I don't know." Nora's words were muffled against Jack's chest.

After a time, when the sobbing subsided, Nora eased herself away from Jack. Moonlight caught the twin rivers of tears on Nora's face. She was beautiful even in sadness. Jack touched her face, traced a channel back to a bruise beneath her left eye.

"What happened?" Jack said.

Nora wrapped her fingers around Jack's hand, eased it away from the bluish skin.

"Sister Freeman caught me taking pictures of the girls' bruises," Nora swallowed, "she took the camera."

"She did this?"

Nora nodded.

"I'm sorry. I should have been with you."

"No. No more apologies."

Nora wiped her face dry.

"Come on. We don't need to be here," Jack said.

"I can't leave. Not yet."

Nora's eyes were bright, stealing starlight from the night sky. Jack saw her anger, her determination. It wasn't over. His heart quickened.

"We're going," Jack said.

"Not without Ellen."

"We'll go to the 'papers, or the police, and come back for her."

"No."

"This has to stop. We can't do any more."

"We have to take her with us. If we leave it could be too late."

Jack sighed and pulled himself free from Nora, a sudden heat worming inside him.

"We can't save everyone."

"Not everyone. *Ellen*. I'm afraid Coyne will hurt her."

"Nora—"

"You don't see him with her. The way he looks at her. The way he..." Nora sniffed, blinked back tears.

Jack moved into the dark beneath a tall pine. He leaned his forehead against the trunk, pressed his shaking hands into the rough bark, felt the ridges bite into his skin.

They matter.

He dragged in a deep breath of sweet night.

"They matter," Jack whispered the words, his lips brushing the bark.

"Then help me."

He turned to Nora. She stood resolute. Luminescent in the pale light of the moon. He saw her strength. Found it fed his own.

"What do we do?"

CHAPTER THREE

They waited beneath the pines until the windows of the hospital were mostly dark. Only a few lights remained, their stark, sterile glow seeping from the huge windows into the night. Jack and Nora noted those still lit. The day rooms of each floor. The nurse stations on the east side of the female wards. A couple of rooms they couldn't name for sure. Perhaps an office or the small infirmary. They waited, huddled together, until the shouting and screaming which accompanied lights-out subsided.

It took a couple of minutes for Jack and Nora to reach the far side of the east wing where they found a door held open with a small stone.

"Was this you?" Jack said. "Jesus."

"We needed a way inside without being seen."

"How did you know I would help?"

"I didn't," Nora said, "But I hoped you would."

Inside, Jack and Nora passed through a dark office and climbed the stairs to the second floor.

The landing was bathed in a greenish glow from a single light on the wall, the grimy dome covering the bulb now a graveyard for decades of trapped insects. To their right, a door with a small, rectangular window permitted access to one of the female wards.

Nora moved to the small pane and peered inside.

"It's clear," Nora said.

She stepped away from the glass, motioned for Jack to look.

"Which room is Ellen's?" Jack asked.

"Cell four."

Jack noted the gentle correction in Nora's words. There were no rooms in Hethpool Grange. Only Cells. Jack looked at the shadows on the linoleum floor cast by the bars on the windows. This was not a place to get better, but to be forgotten.

"Come on," Nora said.

At Ellen's cell, Nora wasted no time in easing open the bolt latch of the peephole, slowly and silently. Jack surveyed the length of the ward painted in shades of blue by the moonlight. They were still alone.

"She's not here," Nora said, "she's gone."

"Gone?"

Jack looked through the small hatch in the door, blinked at the crumpled pile of sheets on the dirty mattress. Beads of sweat traced the ridges of his spine.

"Coyne has her," Nora said.

"You don't know that."

"He took her."

Nora marched towards the central body of the hospital.

"What are you doing?"

Nora turned, gaze intense, sharpened with a determination Jack didn't think he had ever known.

"This stops tonight," Nora said.

Jack envied her strength and willed for some of his own as he and Nora left the east wing and entered the belly of the beast.

***

Coyne's office was empty.

A single lamp lit the room; the light beneath a green, glass shade casting angular shadows into the corners. The window opposite the door reflected their apparitions. In the centre of the room was a huge desk, covered in a mass of papers and open books. Shelves filled with old, well-worn volumes lined the right wall, their titles long gone from the thick leather spines.

"Nora," Jack said, his voice low, "we need to go. *Now*."

"Not until we find Ellen. Help me look."

Jack followed Nora into the office. He pushed the scattered papers around the desk, unsure what he was actually looking for, and uncovered an open book. He flipped the book closed, ran a thumb over gold words. *The Kin of Apep*. The other volumes on the desk were in various states of ruin. *The Restless & Crooked. Vasselin. The Claptrap Manifesto. Bestiarum Vocabulum.* Many in a language he couldn't understand.

A loud pop broke the quiet.

Nora hunched over a small drawer with a letter opener, a tiny gold lock on the inside of it twisted at an awkward angle.

"Jesus," Nora said, "I found it."

She held a leather-bound book.

Coyne's journal. There was no mistaking it. The book he carried around the hospital, scribbling into the pages as he observed the patients. An unease squeezed Jack's chest, made his breathing shallow, weak.

"What now?" Jack said.

Nora ignored him. She opened the book, leafed through the pages.

Jack watched her face contort at the horrors in front of her.

***

Jack read what he could of the pencilled notes over Nora's shoulder as she turned the pages, quickly, as if the words there were toxic.

It is no small wonder to watch the essence of a patient slip away as one performs a leucotomy. Feel the faint resistance of the blade as it glides through living brain tissue...

Another page.

...What do they glimpse in those moments? Their childish God? No. It cannot be something so small. There are powers against his powers...

The text was methodical. Paragraphs broken by names.

...They speak of worlds pushing into one another...

So many names. Names Jack was beginning to recognise.

...inside those monoliths, in the midst of life and death, between the teeth of Charon...

The pages were thinning. Jack knew what was coming. He laid a hand on Nora's shoulder.

"Stop," Jack said.

But it was too late.

Strickland, Peter

It was transformative, somehow, to see the light drain from the boy's eyes down between the stones...

"What is this?"

Sister Freeman stood in the doorway of Coyne's office, face glowing with rage.

A wave of nausea passed through Jack.

"Sister Freeman," Nora said.

"What are you doing in here?" Sister Freeman said.

"Sister..." Jack fumbled for an explanation. An apology.

"What are you doing with *that*?"

She jabbed a finger at the journal in Nora's hands.

"Did you know about this?" Nora said.

"You both need to leave. Now."

"Do you know what Coyne is doing?"

"Mind yourself, girl."

Sister Freeman glared at them, eyes dark and callous.

"Oh God." A deep fury emanated from Nora, forced a quiver into her voice. Jack could almost feel the heat of it against his skin as she passed him and moved closer to Sister Freeman. "You knew. These people needed help and you did nothing. You allowed him to do this."

"Doctor Coyne is helping the people here."

"He's *killing* them."

Nora pushed the book against Sister Freeman, held it against her chest. The older woman stared resolutely at Nora for a moment before her courage deserted her. It was almost imperceptible, like a hairline fracture in bone china, but Jack saw the change, the delicate release of tension in her face.

"Nora," Jack said.

She ignored him, took a step closer to Sister Freeman so their faces were only inches apart.

"He won't fuck you. No matter what you do for him. All the lies in the world won't make him see you as anything other than a twisted, old bitch."

"Please," Sister Freeman closed her eyes, pressed herself against the doorframe. "I didn't know."

"Liar. Where is Ellen?"

Sister Freeman looked at Jack, back to Nora, eyes wide and pleading.

"The chapel," Sister Freeman said, her voice weak and pathetic.

"The chapel?" Jack said. "It's been sealed off for years."

Sister Freeman shook her head.

"No. Doctor Coyne still uses it. For..." she stuttered, "Spiritual Therapy."

"Jesus," Ellen said.

They left Sister Freeman crumpled on the floor of Coyne's office, her quiet sobbing following them down the dark corridor as they left her alone with her sins.

***

Jack and Nora stopped outside of the chapel without a word, communicating instead through their shared fear of what they might find on the other side of the door. Nora let out a shaking breath, pulled her hand from the pocket of her tunic, revealed Coyne's letter opener. She offered it up to Jack. He closed his hand around hers, tightening her grip on the dull blade.

"No," Jack said.

"I don't know if I could use it."

"You don't need to. You just need the threat of it."

"What about you?"

Jack smiled, lips tight and thin on his face.

"I'll be fine."

Something had changed between them since leaving Coyne's office. In the few, silent minutes it had taken them to reach the chapel they had become closer. Entwined by something darker than love, fused together by the secrets of Hethpool Grange.

"What is it?" Nora asked.

"Nothing. I love you. That's all."

Jack knew then he would spend his life with this woman—share the darkness as well as the light, live together in the grey—if she would have him.

CHAPTER FOUR

There were no windows in the chapel. Instead, mosaic frescos of biblical scenes had been painted on the walls and lit by small sconces below. The bulbs still working revealed the crude, flaking images of the Last Supper, The Crucifixion, the Garden of Eden. A wooden crucifix on the wall, framed by creeping rivulets of rainwater seeping through the ceiling, hung high above a dark, black opening in the floor. It might have been a secret door once, but the door was now gone and revealed a narrow stairway. The faint and distant thrum of a motor vibrated beneath their feet. Cool air, sweet with the smell of petrol, came from the passage. The growling engine louder.

Jack took the first few steps, then took out his lighter and snapped it open. The flame shuddered for a moment then settled into a tiny bauble of light. He took a final look at Nora and slipped into the black hole.

***

It was warmer beneath the hospital. Sweat trickled down Jack's spine, the fingers of his free hand traced damp, uneven streaks through the grime on the walls. After several minutes in the dark, he saw a faint, far off light flicker at the end of the tunnel. Jack flicked his lighter closed and buried it deep in his pocket. They edged forward, navigating the uneven ground with deliberate steps, Nora's hand on Jack's shoulder the entire time. It was comforting to feel her warmth, to know she was with him beneath the earth. A balm for the disturbed thumping of his heart.

The light brightened and the roaring motor grew louder as the walls of the tunnel widened into a cavern. Coyne stood in the centre, his back to Jack and Nora. Ellen sat in a large chair, thick leather straps tight around her wrists and ankles, her throat and forehead. Something was jammed in her mouth. A small generator vibrated by the chair, like the beating heart of a giant monster, giving life to a single bulb inside a wire cage.

"Let her go, Coyne," Nora shouted over the sound of the engine.

Coyne twisted, his surprise at finding Jack and Nora in this secret place lasting only a moment. His features narrowed, sharpened into a predatory glare.

"Like peas in a pod," Coyne said, "where one goes, the other must surely follow."

The deep rumbling and dense fumes from the generator pulsed around Jack. The cavern a wasp's nest filled with noise and poison. He blinked, tried to clear his buzzing head, and became aware of the stone monoliths. Five of them, forming a loose circle in the shadows of the chamber. Four were of a similar height, their tips fading into the darkness above. The fifth was smaller, but still loomed behind Ellen and the doctor.

"What is this?" Nora said. The same question stuck on Jack's tongue.

Coyne sneered.

"*Therapy*."

"You're psychotic."

"I prefer enlightened."

Jack shifted his weight and inched closer to Nora, finding comfort, strength, in the heat of her body against his.

"We are not leaving without Ellen," Jack said.

"*It* speaks."

"Untie her."

Jack moved closer to Coyne. The light caught something in the doctor's fist.

"Easy now," Coyne said.

A sliver of metal poked from Coyne's knuckles, narrowing to a razor-sharp point.

An orbitoclast.

Jack knew what it was used for. Remembered Pete's dead, bloodied eyes.

"We know Pete didn't kill himself," Jack swallowed, "you lobotomised him."

"Not for nothing."

"Why?"

"You couldn't begin to understand," Coyne said, moving away from Ellen, closer to the generator and the pool of white light.

"We found your journal."

"Where is it?"

"We have it," Nora said.

"Liar," Coyne glared at them, his eyes wide and dead, impossible to read.

We have it. Jack repeated Nora's words. *We have it*. Tried to dredge up some show of strength so as not to betray the woman he loved. *We have it*.

Coyne shook his head, almost imperceptible, then dropped his gaze.

"There is another world," Coyne said, "and I have glimpsed its shores."

"It's done," Jack said.

"No," Coyne looked at Jack, smiled, "not by a long shot."

Coyne stooped to the generator and slammed his fist into the controls.

Oh god.

The bulb faded.

"Jack," Nora said.

The silence and the dark were absolute.

***

Shit. Shit. Shit.

Indistinct sounds, like the scraping and shuffling of an unseen animal, enveloped Jack, their origins buried in echoes. He pulled out his lighter and thumbed the teeth of the wheel, a small flame illuminating his tiny portion of the cavern. He sensed movement again, a soft displacement of air, then Nora was by him, warm fingers on his arm.

"Where is he?" Nora whispered.

Jack squinted into the gloom. He couldn't see Coyne. He couldn't see anything. He thought of the doctor, hunched and watching from the darkness.

"He's still down here," Jack said. Only seconds could have passed since the light went out. "Keep an eye out."

Ellen materialised from the dark like a phantom. Eyes bulging, orange in the naked flame. Her forehead glistened with a fine sheen of sweat.

"It's okay, Ellen," Nora said, "we're here."

Jack set the lighter on the floor and pulled the gag, dark and sodden, from Ellen's mouth.

"He...He..." Ellen sucked in a breath, coughed.

"Don't talk," Jack put a hand on Ellen's shoulder, "we'll get you out."

He worked quickly, unbuckling the leather restraint around Ellen's forehead first. Ellen's head lolled forward, and she spat a wad of blood into her lap. Jack moved through the remaining restraints, releasing each heavy clasp with deft familiarity. With the last strap loosened, Jack stooped to lift the lighter.

"Thank..." Ellen stopped.

Jack raised the light, followed Ellen's glassy stare.

Nora stood rigid, her limbs stiff, wrought with a violent tension. A sudden, thin flash of reflected light came from the deeper dark behind her.

"*Nora.*"

Jack reached out as the shining blade vanished into Nora's abdomen.

***

Nora screamed, the sound deafening in the underground night.

Jack cried out her name as she fell into a heap at his feet. The flame in his hand flickered, caught in a rush of cold air, then Coyne was on Jack and the two men were falling.

The unforgiving earth caught Jack and crushed the air from his lungs.

It was coffin dark. The lighter was gone.

Jack heaved in a stifled breath as Coyne fell upon him. Jack grabbed and pushed at the doctor, fingers slipping against cloth and flesh, unable to find purchase. Something sharp stabbed into the meat of his right shoulder, the agonising needle tore through the muscle and scraped bone. Jack wailed through gritted teeth as Coyne pulled the orbitoclast free. He felt his flesh sucking at the weapon, resisting its exit. Jack grabbed at the blaze in his shoulder, pressed his fingers into his hot blood. Above him, Coyne shrieked.

"Bitch," Coyne said.

Jack felt the doctor move—thought Coyne might be trying to stand—and tried to crawl free. He grabbed at the damp earth, legs twisting and bucking. He heard movement all around him, sensed the shifting of bodies in the pitch black.

There was another howl, raw and pained.

Coyne was no longer on him. Jack pushed himself to his knees, the pain in his shoulder flaring with the exertion.

"Whore," Coyne said, his voice a guttural hiss, "you fucking whore."

There was a soft rasp to Jack's right and a single flame bloomed.

Nora was on her knees, holding his lighter aloft. Her other hand pressed hard against her stomach, fingers slick with oozing blood which shone in the light of the naked flame.

"Nora—"

"Okay," Nora panted, "I'm okay."

"We need to get help," Ellen said.

Ellen was trembling, face and hair spattered with a fine spray of blood, the short, blunt blade clenched tight in her crimson fist.

The letter opener.

Coyne lay at her feet. A thick pool of black gore soaking the earth beneath him. Jack watched the doctor's bloody chest, waited for the labored rise and fall, some sign of life.

There was nothing.

"He's dead," Jack said.

"I didn't mean to kill him. I didn't. He was—I didn't know how else to stop him," Ellen said.

"You," Nora winced, "you had no choice."

"We need to go," Jack said, standing. "Ellen, help Nora."

As the women moved towards the tunnel, Ellen supporting Nora, Jack slipped deeper into the shadows and found the bulky shape of the generator. He stooped, picked up the jerry can and shook it, listened to the liquid slosh inside.

Enough.

"What are you doing?" Nora said.

"We're burning this place down," Jack said, unscrewing the cap from the petrol tank, "all of it."

"Jack—"

"He's dead. Whatever he's done, whatever happened here, this wasn't how it was supposed to end."

Jack shook the can, dousing the generator and the earth at his feet with petrol.

"Wait," Nora said, wincing at a fresh twist of pain in her stomach. She was hurt. Badly. Jack needed to act quickly.

"Ellen, get her out of here."

Jack backed out of the chamber after the women, leaving a trail of fuel as he went. The splashes and pools in his wake, all metallic greens and purples, glistened in the fading light. He lingered by Coyne's body, poured a little more freely near the swelling pool of blood, used the last of the fuel to trace his retreat to the tunnel.

Nora and Ellen waited for him in the passage. Without a word he took the lighter from Ellen and kneeled to the shining stream leading off into the chamber.

"Go," Jack shouted.

Nora and Ellen did, their footsteps receding behind Jack. He used his free hand to wipe the sweat from his brow, lowered the lighter to the thin line of petrol by his foot.

A blue flame jumped into life and quickly snaked into the darkness, exploding into a blaze of yellow light inside the cave. A rush of searing air slammed into Jack, pushed him against the wall. He watched long shadows cast by the stones dance for a brief moment before the arcane display was blotted out by smoke.

It was then the screaming started.

Jack stared into the flames. He tried to locate the doctor amongst the fire and smoke but found nothing except violent brightness, intense heat. He cried out for Coyne but all that came back were screams. Thick tendrils of black fog began to choke Jack, forcing him back from the blaze. There was no way back into the chamber.

The guttural shrieking within the fire finally broke and gave way to a terrible, sickly laughter.

What have I done?

***

Jack took the steps from the earth two at a time, emerging into the chapel in a cloud of thin, grey smoke. Ellen and Nora stared at him, faces ashen, haunted by the nightmare sounds from below.

"He was dead," Jack said, his voice quiet, trembling, "I couldn't get to him. I thought he was gone. I thought he was already dead."

"We all know what he did," Nora said.

"But," Jack gagged involuntarily.

"We had no choice. He would have killed all of us," Nora said. "He tried to kill me."

Nora took his hand and squeezed, her fingers slick with blood. *Her blood.* The syrupy warmth against his palm roused Jack, broke the disgusted malaise which gripped him.

"We need to get help," Jack said, "Ellen, go find—"

"Wait," Nora said, "listen to me. Everything that happened was an accident."

"Nora—"

"It was an accident."

Jack saw Ellen nod in the gloom; shattered eyes sunken in her gaunt face. He imagined he looked much the same. Tired. Broken.

"An accident," Jack said. "Now we need to go find some help."

Something exploded below the earth and expelled a thunderous roar which shook the ground beneath their feet.

***

A greasy fog engulfed Jack, Nora and Ellen as they left the chapel and slipped into a corridor of Hethpool Grange.

The shrill ringing of a fire alarm started seconds after the earthquake. The explosion—the flames must have reached the fuel tank of the generator—brought fire to the surface. An eruption from hell. Jack wondered how far underground the tunnel wound, what might stand above the chamber. The dark was disorientating. He had no way of knowing where they might have been.

"We have to help with the evacuation," Nora said.

She lay against the wall, hands clasped to her wound. Her breathing was laboured, her hair had fallen from the bun and loose curls stuck to her face.

"Don't be stupid," Ellen said. "You're in no fit state."

"She's right," Jack said.

"I have to." Nora pushed herself upright and stumbled against Ellen.

"Enough," Jack said, an unfamiliar edge in his voice. Sharp, ready to cut. He could see from the way Nora looked at him, as though he were a stranger, it wounded her. He looked away from her glistening eyes, found Ellen. "Get her out of the hospital. Keep pressure on the wound. I'll go help with the evacuation."

CHAPTER FIVE

Patients were filing down the stairs of the west wing and into the large foyer where Tommy, one of the attendants, was urging them outside. The line moved steadily, shuffling after one another out into the night where they gathered in the gardens and turned to look at the burning hospital like a mob of restless ghouls.

"Male wards are clear," Tommy shouted.

"What about east wing?" Jack said.

"Cleared."

"Where did the fire start?"

"Tip of the wing. An explosion beneath the airing yard. The roof is ablaze."

Violent patients.

No one was housed there, hadn't been in all the time Jack worked at Hethpool Grange. It was mostly forgotten. The squeezing fear in Jack's chest loosened, the weight shifted. He breathed deeply, skin tingling with warm relief.

"You saw Coyne? Sister Freeman?" Tommy asked.

"No."

It was all Jack could manage.

***

The third floor was deserted. The chaos of the evacuation a world away. Even the amber glow of dancing flame reflecting in the tall windows of the hall was serene.

A chill wind stopped Jack in the doorway of Coyne's office. The window was open, offering a perfect square of night. The cold air, faintly perfumed with burning wood, prickled his skin as he took careful steps into the empty room.

The journal lay on the floor beneath the window, pages flapping in the breeze. Jack grabbed the flaking pane and leaned out into the night. He knew what he would find below the mystery, so mundane, so simple, already solved—yet he felt compelled to look.

Sister Freeman lay in the grass, dead eyes staring up at him.

Before leaving the office, Jack picked up Coyne's journal, tucked it into the waistband of his trousers, the shape hidden beneath his loose top. The book felt dirty against his skin. He had a sudden urge to burn the thing, to watch the pages blacken, see the words reduced to ash. But it was those same words which stopped him. Those words were all that remained of Coyne and the suffering he had inflicted. The only surviving record of his victims. They deserved so much more than the brutality they received at Coyne's hands. They deserved more than fire. They deserved to survive Hethpool Grange.

Even if it was only in name.

***

The night outside the hospital was incandescent.

The fire, so bright it was almost white, slowly devoured the interior of the west wing making the century old walls look like a paper silhouette. Flames licked from the shattered windows, blackening the thick brick. Great clouds of charcoal smoke bulged from the open roof and blossomed in the sky above.

There were people everywhere, staff and patients alike, heads craned to the sight before them. Mesmerised by the blaze, bodies perfectly still, faces serene. The only noise the unbroken sound of burning, like an incessant roll of thunder never reaching a crescendo.

Jack wandered amongst the crowd in the garden, looking for Nora and Ellen in the brief moments the allure of the flames faltered, for he too felt the pull of fire.

"Jack," Ellen said, "here."

Ellen was on her knees by Nora, who lay on the earth. Ellen held her hands to the wound in Nora's stomach, her fingers bloody. Nora's eyes were closed, but her eyelids fluttered, as though she were dreaming.

Jack fell to his knees beside her.

"Nora? Can you hear me?" Jack said.

"She's unconscious."

A male voice behind Jack.

"Will she be okay?" Jack said without turning.

"She's lost a lot of blood." The voice authoritative. Noncommittal.

Jack pressed a palm against Nora's cheek, leaned in close to her, pressed his lips against her ear.

"I'm sorry. If you can hear me, I'm sorry. You hang on, okay? I don't want to do any of this without you. I love you."

Jack took Nora's hand when he heard the distant wail of sirens and did not let go until the hospital, the devouring fire, the rising columns of smoke visible for miles against a clear blue dawn, became nothing but memory.

CHAPTER SIX

Jack slipped home briefly—after several reassurances from the doctors that Nora would pull through—to scrub the sweat and charcoal stink from his skin. On his return to the hospital, he resumed his vigil at Nora's bedside where he read Coyne's journal. He absorbed the words in the low light, ran his fingers over the names of the dead, tried to make sense of the seething madness on those brittle pages.

Two days later, Nora awoke, and they started their lives together.

***

There were questions regarding Hethpool Grange and the fire, but no one pushed too hard for answers, not when they indicated years of abuse unnoticed by the same people now asking the questions. It was better to close ranks and smother the truth, talk of national failings and reform. Patients were quietly moved to other facilities or introduced back into the community.

The newspapers were interested for approximately three days, then Lord Denning published his report on the Profumo Affair. The stories told by survivors became hearsay, a morbid curiosity, and Hethpool Grange became a paltry footnote in history.

Ellen gave birth to a son in the spring of 1964. On the birth certificate she listed the father as Peter Strickland.

Jack and Nora tried desperately for a family of their own, but the injury Nora sustained at Coyne's hand meant the child they longed for never came.

Sometimes Jack wondered if this was punishment for what he had done.

Miracles, he reasoned, were for the good.

They stopped trying for a baby. They stopped talking of Coyne, the fire, the hospital entirely. Jack never knew the reason for Nora's silence, but he knew the reason for his own. It all hurt too much.

Time passed like a dream and, for the most part, the years were kind. Those years soon became decades, isolating those black memories of Hethpool Grange.

Still, in those deathly quiet moments, when the nights stretched impossibly long and sleep eluded Jack, visions of the fire returned and he was lost to the dark shadows reaching out of the past.

PART THREE: ASH - 2020

CHAPTER ONE

"What the hell is happening?" Dani said. Her voice barely a whisper.

Jack pulled his ear away from the door, from the perfect silence beyond the small office. Dani stood with her back to the window, framed by the ash outside, still falling like sickly snow. She crossed her arms tightly in an effort to still her trembling, but it was no use. Ellen, resting in a molding chair, looked from Dani to Jack.

"Stop doing that." Dani squeezed the words out between pursed lips.

"What?" Ellen said.

"Looking at each other like that."

"Dani—"

"Every time I say something, or ask something, you two look at each other like kids caught with their hand in the biscuit barrel. Something is wrong here. Seriously wrong."

"We need to keep quiet," Ellen said. "Just while we figure this out."

"You both need to tell me what the fuck is going on."

Jack saw the fear rising inside Dani, threatening to spill out of her in great, screaming waves.

"We will. *I* will. As best as I can at least," Jack said.

Dani ran her hands over her face, pulled them through her hair and laid them to rest on the back of her neck. She took a deep breath and, as she let it go, Jack saw some of the tension slip from her shoulders.

"Coyne," Jack said. "Everything. All of it. It starts and ends with Coyne."

***

Jack spoke quietly and succinctly, like a man in confession. Only there would be no forgiveness for what he had done. He did not expect or want it. He thought he would falter, choke on the fundamental truth which had haunted him for almost fifty years, but he found the words with ease.

His truth, however atrocious, was uncomplicated.

Once Jack finished speaking of the fire, his responsibility for Coyne's death, he fell silent. There was no catharsis, just the familiar misery. A torment, decades old. Jack expected scorn or disgust from Dani, but instead he saw only sadness in her eyes.

"Why didn't you tell me any of this?" Dani said to Ellen.

"Because I was afraid of what it would mean if I did. I worried if you found out about this place, what happened...we made some terrible choices," Ellen said.

"I was the one who killed him, Ellen. This isn't on you," Jack said.

Ellen ignored Jack and took one of Dani's hands in hers.

"I thought if you knew what we did, learned what I am, then I would lose you," Ellen said.

"Neither of you had a choice. I love you, Nanna," Dani said. She pulled Ellen into an embrace.

Jack found the gesture alien inside a place so devoid of human compassion. After a moment, the women seemed to sense the same strangeness and separated.

"None of that explains this," Dani said, gesturing to the window, to the ash.

"No," Jack agreed.

"Is," Dani swallowed and retried the difficult question. "Was that a ghost?"

"I think it's worse," Jack said, "much worse. Coyne kept a journal. It listed his victims, those he lobotomised below ground. Coyne had them describe what they saw as they died. They spoke of another world. Every one of them."

"What?" Dani said.

"Those stones I mentioned, Coyne said standing amongst them was to stand in the palm of a god and he used the lobotomies to communicate with it. He saw the other world as a way to exist beyond death."

"So, this place, it's like a door? One world pushing against another?"

"Yes."

"How do we close it?"

"I don't know."

A cold fear settled into the marrow of Jack's bones and, with it, came a rich pain. Shards of glass deep within his shoulder, reopening an ancient wound. The past and present somehow fused now he was back inside Hethpool Grange.

"We need to leave," Ellen said.

"What if he follows us?" Dani said.

"He won't," Jack said.

"Why?"

"I'm not sure, but," Jack rubbed absently at the ache, "somehow I think he's bound to this place."

"He would have come for us had he been able," Ellen said. "This place, it's his own personal hell."

***

Jack, Ellen and Dani moved quickly through the old halls, careful not to disturb the debris beneath their feet. The rooms and corridors, lost to almost fifty years of rot and ruin, stood dormant, reduced to some obscene likeness of a time long ago.

Through the high, barred windows inside the dining hall, Jack noticed the light outside was fading. He checked his watch. It was not yet noon.

"Look," Ellen said.

She was not looking at the rising darkness as Jack suspected, but down at her hands.

"Are you okay?" Dani said.

Ellen rubbed the thumb of one hand over the wrist of the other. Even in the waning light Jack could make out the red impressions on Ellen's arms.

"I'm fine, it's just..."

Ellen touched her fingers to the thick band of inflamed skin around her neck, as thick as a belt.

Or a restraint.

"My shoulder—" Jack stopped, the air around him thick with the bitter scent of burning.

"If only I'd hit your heart, Jacky-boy."

CHAPTER TWO

Coyne stood in the doorway at the far side of the room, wrapped in smoke and ash. It hurt to look at the fire writhing inside Coyne's blackened husk, to gaze into the golden flames deep in the sockets of the doctor's eyes.

"You need to go. *Now,*" Jack said.

Dani took Ellen by the arm and the three of them hurried towards a door in the near wall. They did not dare look back at Coyne, only chased their own shadows, spawned from the doctor's light.

***

Jack followed the women through the gloom, Ellen pointing the way to Dani until they came to the foyer.

Glancing back, Jack saw dancing fire and shadow swell and grow from a bend at the end of the hall, steadily but without urgency. Coyne was toying with them, enjoying the hunt.

I can feel him inside my head.

I feel it calling to me.

The talons of Hethpool Grange were deeper than will and reason. Even if they did escape, something would reach out from this place and pull him back. Pull Ellen back.

The women covered their mouths, ready to step out into the ash storm then Ellen turned to Jack.

"Go," Jack said.

"What are you doing?" Ellen said.

"Why are we here? Something made us come. Even if we leave—"

"But."

"—we'll still end up back here."

"Jack?" Dani said.

He turned to her, tried to smile.

"Get to the car and drive away from this place," Jack said. "I'll be right behind you."

The women hesitated. Their eyes perfect echoes of one another's, filled with the same sadness and resignation.

"Go," Jack said.

He did not wait for Ellen and Dani to disappear into the swirling grey outside. Did not utter a farewell. There was no time for sentiment. He put his back to the women, the world beyond this place, and hurried into the heart of Hethpool Grange once more.

***

There was only one place Jack could go.

He moved as quickly as his old muscles would allow, the used-up meat in his joints screaming as he tried to muster the almost forgotten notion of a jog. His breathing was ragged, the air in his lungs thick and wet with decay. The pain in his shoulder intensified. Jack could feel the scar tissue tearing open.

The darkness of the place did not slow Jack. He kicked aside rotten wood and shattered tiles, threw his body into the doors still clinging desperately to their old hinges. For too long the hospital had stood in silence. The noise he now made was substantial. Real. A trail of sound for Coyne to chase.

Jack pushed his way into the chapel, wiped the stinging sweat from his eyes and took in the small room. On the far wall where a crucifix once hung were four words, scratched in soot.

HERE

I

AM

GOD

Jack spat out a mouthful of sour mucus coughed up from his burning lungs. He dragged in a breath, willed his failing body not to give in, not yet.

As Jack descended into the earth, he kept his eyes fixed on the epitaph and hoped it was not true.

***

At the bottom of the steps, Jack stretched his arms to the walls of the tunnel and pressed his palms against the cool earth. The dark surrounding him was absolute. He edged forward, dragging his feet over the ground so as not to trip over some unseen object, feeling his way through the dark towards the stone circle.

The steady rhythm of his boots scraping against the stone comforted him. His breathing slowed, his heart stopped hammering and, after a time, he let his eyes close. He navigated by touch alone and, as he wandered the passage, so too did his mind.

***

Jack was in Nora's room at the hospice. He could smell the rain on his coat, the lilies by her bedside, the disinfectant beneath it all. He lay

Nora's hand in his palm, cupped it like a tiny bird, scared even a gentle squeeze might shatter her brittle bones. The cancer had eaten most of Nora, reduced her to a husk. Their time on this earth was almost up. But there was still warmth in her hand and for that Jack was thankful.

"I don't want to do this without you," Jack said.

He kissed the tips of Nora's fingers.

"I'm sorry, but you're going to have to."

"I hope—"

"What?"

"I hope I made you happy."

Nora smiled and Jack began to cry.

"The happiest."

"You're everything. You know that?"

"I do," Nora said. "Now, let me sleep. Let me dream of us."

An hour later Nora was gone.

***

The walls beneath Jack's fingers were moving further apart. The tunnel widening. He opened his eyes slowly, loathe to leave even the bleakest memory of Nora. He expected the inky black to envelope him, but found the darkness was fading. He could make out the shape of the tunnel around him. Barely, but it was there. The walls lit with spectral light.

The stones were close.

Jack began to run.

CHAPTER THREE

Jack emerged from the tunnel and found himself standing in a huge a crater. The chamber was gone. The roof brought down in the generator explosion. The ash, falling from the bleak sky overhead, coated everything in an anaemic dust. Still standing tall amongst the rubble, untouched by the explosion, were the five stones.

The palm of a god.

Jack scrambled up a mound of rock, navigated the uneven terrain until he stood in the centre of the crater. He looked around at the stones stretching out of the pit, thinking perhaps they intended to pull down the charcoal sky above.

He stooped, pulled a length of rusting pipe from the rubble at his feet.

This is where it ends.

The wound in Jack's shoulder ached, bleeding freely now. He noted the dark stain soaking through his jacket, the thin, crimson rivulets on his hand. He tightened his grip on the pipe, without conviction.

HERE I AM GOD.

The wind screamed down from the heavens and stirred the spectral ash of a fire long ago as Jack waited for Coyne.

***

Golden light lit the mouth of the tunnel. Faint at first, no brighter than a solitary candle, finally swelling into a bright and hungry blaze.

Coyne—a charred shadow, cloaked in licking flame—emerged into the pit.

Intense fear seized Jack, spread through his body like a poison, fusing his muscles to leaden bones. He could not move. There was nowhere left to go.

"*So, here we are,*" Coyne said.

Jack was silent.

"*This is some poetry,*" Coyne began to climb the mound towards Jack, "*that we should end up here.*"

"I know how many you killed," Jack said.

"*Saved. How many I saved.*"

"I know their names. Every one of them. I have your journal."

There was no way to read Coyne's burning features, but Jack thought he saw the doctor's eyes, those pits of fire, narrow.

"*Then you know what this place is.*"

"A door." Jack's voice trembled.

A roar of scorched laughter came from Coyne.

"*A door is a practical notion. A tangible object with an obvious purpose. This place is much more delicate.*"

Coyne was closer now, only a few short meters lay between them. Jack could feel the heat coming from the thing before him. He raised the pipe, seized it with both hands.

"Stop."

There was no strength in Jack's voice, no power in his command, but Coyne remained where he was.

"*Do you see it, Jacky-boy? The shore of that other world?*"

Jack took a small step backwards, steadied his feet against the uneven rock beneath him.

"When you left me for dead, burned me alive between these stones, I saw it. I saw it and I submitted to what dwells there. This state of perpetual death was my reward. I may burn for eternity, but at least I am a god."

"I tried to," Jack swallowed. "The fire—"

Coyne rushed towards Jack. There was no time to swing the pipe, no time to retreat. Jack simply stood there as Coyne stabbed him in the stomach with the orbitoclast. The metal burned inside him.

"Your heart is your failing, Jacky-boy," Coyne screamed.

Jack tried to stumble away from the doctor but was too slow. Coyne grabbed him by the throat. The pain was immediate. Jack opened his mouth to scream but the searing fingers only squeezed tighter. He could smell his flesh burning, heard the skin of his neck sizzling in Coyne's grip. The air in his lungs escaped his mouth in a cloud of vapor. His vision blurred and darkened, the light of some distant fire flickering at the edges.

This is how I die.

Jack choked in a tiny breath, his dry tongue clicking against the roof of his mouth. It was purely instinctive, but his body was fighting and that was something. He focused on the muscles at the back of his throat, tried to form a word, and from the word find something other than terror.

"Nora."

Her name was nothing more than a whisper, lost on the wind, but it was all Jack needed. All he ever needed. Nora had, and always would be, the reason for his strength.

Jack's hand found the orbitoclast in his gut. He wrapped his fingers around the crescent shaped handle, pulled it free, plunged the thin blade deep into Coyne's chest.

***

Coyne let out a fierce scream.

The noose of fire around Jack's throat loosened and he collapsed to his knees. Violent tremors coursed through his body; shock, brought on by the overwhelming agony, raged through every inch of him. He choked down another lungful of hot air, his throat offering up a fractured whine as he did. Jack lifted his head, readied himself for the attack that would inevitably kill him.

They were no longer in the crater.

He was kneeling before a limitless ocean, the water the colour of midnight. The shore stretched endlessly to either side of him, featureless except for the five columns of stone, the monoliths enormous replicas of those beneath Hethpool Grange. In the deep night sky overhead, amongst the diamond white stars, were monstrous, writhing shapes.

"You know you can't help that bitch," Coyne said.

Jack willed himself to stand but the muscles in his legs refused to move. He could only watch his death, one made entirely of fire and shadow, come for him.

Nora.

He repeated her name. A prayer to the dead.

Nora. Nora. Nora.

The flames found Jack's throat once more and he was lifted from the ground.

"*Ellen will return, and when she does, I will be waiting,"* Coyne said.

Jack struggled against the burning vice around his neck, looked down into the hell inside Coyne's eyes.

He is...

Jack punched into the crackling wound in Coyne's chest, withdrew his fist and punched in again, further this time, clawing at the brittle flesh.

"*...no god,"* Jack managed.

With the little strength he had, Jack reached his ruined hands into the cavity, pushed deep, found the beating inferno of Coyne's heart. The meat on Jack's fingers blistered, burst, blistered again as he wrenched the burning coal free.

Then Jack was falling, the stone in his hand cold before he hit the hard earth.

CHAPTER FOUR

The other world—and what dwelled within it—was gone.

Jack lay in the crater. He could no longer feel any pain, only an icy, scouring wind over his broken body. It was the agony in his heart which burned brightest.

Nora was gone.

He would never see her again.

There was no such thing as ghosts.

Jack uttered a single word—a sweet and beautiful prayer for the woman he loved—and slipped into the endless and empty dark of death.

BIOGRAPHY

Grant Longstaff is from Gateshead; a small, suitably dismal town in the north east of England where nothing much happens. He had no choice but to write fiction.

His work has appeared in the Bram Stoker Nominated *Arterial Bloom* (ed. Mercedes M. Yardley), *Shallow Waters Vol. 8* and *Aurealis Magazine* and on *The Other Stories* and *Tales to Terrify* podcasts.

Between the Teeth of Charon is his first solo release.

You can find him on Twitter @GrantLongstaff or at www.grantlongstaff.co.uk

ADRIAN BALDWIN (COVER ARTIST)

Adrian is a Mancunian now living and working in Wales. Back in the 1990s, he wrote for various TV shows/personalities: Smith & Jones, Clive Anderson, Brian Conley, Paul McKenna, Hale & Pace, Rory Bremner (and a few others). Wooo, get him! Since then, he has written three screenplays—one of which received generous financial backing from the Film Agency for Wales. Then along came the global recession which kicked the UK Film industry in the nuts. What a bummer! Not to be outdone, he turned to novel writing—which had always been his real dream—and, in particular, a genre he feels is often overlooked; a genre he has always been a fan of: Dark Comedy (sometimes referred to as Horror's weird cousin). *Barnacle Brat* (a dark comedy for grown-ups), his first novel won Indie Novel of the Year 2016 award; his second novel *Stanley Mccloud Must Die!* (more dark comedy for grown-ups) published in 2016 and his third: *The Snowman And The Scarecrow* (another dark comedy for grown-ups) published in 2018. Adrian Baldwin has also written and published a number of dark comedy short stories. He designs book covers too—not just for his own books but for a growing number of publishers.

For more information on the award-winning author, check out:

https://adrianbaldwin.info/

DEMAIN PUBLISHING

To keep up to-date on all news DEMAIN (including future submission calls and releases) you can follow us in a number of ways:

BLOG:
www.demainpublishingblog.weebly.com

TWITTER:
@DemainPubUk

FACEBOOK PAGE:
Demain Publishing

INSTAGRAM:
demainpublishing

www.ingramcontent.com/pod-product-compliance
Lightning Source LLC
LaVergne TN
LVHW041118150826
845673LV00007B/2110